The Restaurant

Pallavi Chandra

AF657998

BlueRose ONE .com
Stories Matter
NewDelhi • London

BLUEROSE PUBLISHERS
India | U.K.

BlueRose ONE
Stories Matter
New Delhi • London

For permissions requests or inquiries regarding this publication, please contact:

BLUEROSE PUBLISHERS
www.BlueRoseONE.com
info@bluerosepublishers.com
+91 8882 898 898
+4407342408967

ISBN: 978-93-6783-372-8

Cover design: Shubham Verma
Typesetting: Sagar

First Edition: February 2025

Acknowledgment

I want to dedicate this poignant tale of three women to all of "us" who work in confinement and silence. For centuries, women have been fighting for their rights, and the right to freedom of choice, and they will keep fighting. Women, like men, have dreams and aspirations that are suppressed under the umbrella of patriarchy. Of course, this is not the first book nor is it going to be the last book in this series of women's choices and their suffocation as bonded laborers. But the stories need to be told from time to time so that the coming generations do not forget the struggles, the miseries, the constant shattering of dreams.

The cycle of women's lives keeps on reminding women, sooner or later, that they belong to the kitchen nurturing and taking care of the family. The

Restaurant is an abstract representation of this belongingness. Indeed the acceptance helped them carry the wisdom of cooking as a tradition, but it has also created an endless circular chain for these women.

The ugly patriarchal norms of society have divorced them from their own true identity. This identity crisis often makes them invisible. I have always wondered why our mothers, aunts, and sisters would pause for a bit to answer: "What is your favorite food?" The question will be singular, yet the answer…needs a pause. Tales like these highlight the compromises they have made regarding their preferences, aspirations, and desires, ultimately leading them to surrender their autonomy and become "enslaved" by the demands of patriarchy.

For ages, women and their sacrifices have gone unnoticed in the so-called civilized society while they continue to enjoy autonomy in traditional societies. A credit long due… The tale of these three women, Mirzya, Natalie, and Derora, reminds us of our silent struggles and sacrifices.

The story of these three women is shrouded in silence and calmness reflecting the characteristics of a woman which is usually a part of our conditioning. The emotions swirling inside these three women remained intact deep within them, only to pursue persistence and hope to overcome their fate and end their miseries. The narrative centers on Mirzya, a mother of three, who struggles to chase her dreams; Natalie, a single mother in an unfamiliar land, trying to navigate her challenges to raise her son; and Derora, an illiterate woman who attempts to escape her harsh reality, only to find herself ensnared once more in this cycle of bondage. The irony is Natalie felt alienated because she was a 'refugee', but others felt alienated because they were 'women'.

Contents

Ch. 1

The Restaurant as a "She"

"It's 48 New Shekel", Mirzya replied gently while checking the receipt for the order.

She went to the kitchen that was just behind the billing counter and asked for the last order preparation placed for one falafel shawarma.

She picked up her bag, lying on the steel stand. Although the stand was often used to keep loaves of bread, it also served as an apt place for Mirzya's bag. It was at the right-hand distance from the billing counter.

While leaving, Mirzya came near Natalie, looked up at her, smiled, and gave the keys with eyes on her hands. Natalie accepted the keys silently. While leaving, she turned back and said bye to Natalie, who started preparing for the last order of falafel shawarma, giving a very faint smile to Mirzya's goodbye.

Mirzya ran the restaurant which she inherited from her father. When she took over the restaurant, she was not in proper condition. The business was also slow. She worked hard to make the restaurant a household name in the community. She, now, was selling shakshuka, musabbaha, shawarmas, kebabs, hummus, pita, tabbouleh, couscous, and other Mediterranean cuisines at a relatively lower price than others. The restaurant also offered tea with many herbal options depending on the seasons. Tea was often accompanied by famous cookies Ma'amouls. Coffee, although, was usually a breakfast beverage.

She expanded the restaurant from a tiny kitchen cum dining room to a moderate size that can accommodate roughly around 70 people at a time. The restaurant was situated in that part of the city where people from different neighborhoods were doing small businesses. The street, thus, got a colloquial name for itself: sh'khunah, meaning neighborhood. The neighborhood had offered a livelihood for many. Just like Mirzya, women were involved in different kinds of business. They varied from handicrafts to stitching, restaurants to show-pieces, and salons to vegetable shops. The businesses done by women were within the purview of what society always labeled as “women's work”.

Mirzya was a kind woman with passion and dreams. She was bold, at least enough to take a few small risks.

She often battled within herself between modernity and traditionalism. The East European style modern art paintings on the one side of the walls were a testament to her flowing modern thoughts. The Yemini style of the painting on the other side of the wall reflected her love for carrying over the traditions in the form of art and culture. Gazing at the restaurant and Mirzya's calm yet flowing personality, one could have very easily contemplated that she was the designer of “her” restaurant. The design of the chairs and tables was highly influenced by an amalgamation of the European and Yemini styles. Of course, “she” was not a fancy restaurant. Mirzya, particularly, emphasized the homely part, both in ambiance and taste.

The restaurant had a small kitchen straight to the cash counter. The right side of the cash counter had a place for a grill and barbeque. The right from the entrance door also contained counters to collect orders. She kept saying, "People should feel they are being served at their dining table" and kudos to her, she made that happen. The restaurant would witness a long queue from 9:00 am to 3:00 pm.

"She" was a nostalgic place for Mirzya. She would often reminisce about her baba and how she used to visit the restaurant with him. As a child, she would sit in any part of her, doing her homework, or finishing her drawing. Sometimes, helping her father serve the tables.

Mirzya, after waiting at the nearby signal, crossed on green and walked through the pathway. She often used the "bridge road" to go back home.

The "bridge road" was a lesser-known road. It connected the city to the nearby neighborhoods. Although a very busy one, it held the utmost serenity. It was as long as the California bridge, bridging the commotion of the cities with the calmness of neighborhoods including hers. Mirzya's neighborhood was somewhere between a village and a suburb with a community of less than 110 people.

She would often stop by the bridge. The gentle breeze across the bridge produced a piece of melodious music for her ears. It gave her a sense of freedom. There was an assembly of benches on both ends of the bridge. She would sit on one of the benches looking at the incredible sight of the bridge and the river beneath, only to behold. And when the sun sets, she will pick up her bag and will be ready to head back home. Her return home would be accompanied by a void expression on her face, a vivid representation of losing herself. Or perhaps, accepting the harsh realities of life as a woman.

Ch. 2

Home not so Home?

Mirzya reached her house. It was in a small suburb which was exactly 4 miles away from her restaurant.

She opened her home door, kept her shoes, and entered the house. It was already 8:00 pm.

The house was a double-storied building with 3 bedrooms. It was a legacy from her father. The house had a traditional suburban style of architecture. It was decorated in a traditional style. It had a hall that could be seen straight from the entrance. On the left side of the hall was the kitchen. There was a small 6-scater dining table placed at the end of the hall. Right after the entrance was the shoe area with some hooks on the wall where Mirzya often kept her coat. Among all the 3 bedrooms, the downstairs room was the smallest of all, which was also Mirzya's bedroom. Just after the entrance, on the right side, there was a staircase for the upper bedrooms. One room was on the left to the upper staircase which was shared by her kids and the right one was solely for her mother-in-law.

"Jafar is asking for dinner", her mother-in-law said. After hanging her coat, she went straight to the kitchen and started preparing bread.

(Though the distance between the restaurant and home was 4 miles, it usually took Mirzya one hour to reach home. Even upon knowing that she will be questioned, she would prefer an hour delay "caused by" sitting at the bench of the bridge road route to home. She enjoyed the one hour of evening for herself so much that she refrained from giving up.)

At the dinner table, while arranging dishes, she called her three kids: Zenab, Zareen, and Hamid, for food.

She would have prepared bread, chickpea hummus, and chicken alfaham for the family. It was 9:30 pm.

"How were the sales at the restaurant today?" Jafar asked.

"I need to check the receipts." She replied.

"Is it necessary to go to a restaurant? It's too late for dinner." Jafar asked while taking a bite of the bread.

Jafar's mother and her three kids who were still too young to understand, saw her as if all had consented to Jafar's remarks. Jafar's question created an endless silence at the dinner table for the night.

Jafar was a firm man with utmost patriarchal beliefs. He disapproved of Mrizya's going out and working at the restaurant. But she was also firm about running her father's restaurant by herself. The patriarchal belief was evident from the fact that she was supposed to prepare food for the family.

Mirzya, contrary to Jafar's character, was a very compassionate, calm woman with liberal thinking. She would usually remain silent over many of his ideologies and beliefs that she disapproved of.

Ch. 3

The Next Morning

Mirzya closed the house door. She fixed Zenab's school bag and walked with her three kids towards school. She dropped them, waved her hands to say bye to them, adjusted her sling bag properly to her shoulders, and headed towards the restaurant.

On the same morning, there was a loud and hard knock at the door. Natalie opened the door, leaving it ajar. Outside, an old man was standing looking at her.

"Today is 5th", Madam..... I hope you remember, the man said 'Madam…', giving stress to every alphabet.

"I thought it was the 10th", she replied in a sordid tone.

The old man who was known as Kiev replied, "It's the 5th of every month, madam".

Frightened, she went inside and came with money in her hands.

It's 1500 New Shekel for now. I will pay 500 later. Kiev took the money and gave a frowning look before leaving.

She closed the door, put her papers inside the bag, opened the door, and left for work.

"Good morning, Mirzya." Natalie greeted when Mirzya entered the restaurant.

"Today, we have received 6 orders to start with." Natalie counted them all.

"Which… to start with….?" Natalie asked in a very confused, stressful, and feeble tone.

Mirzya saw the tokens and receipts.

"Achot, let's make falafel for Abiram's uncle first." She smiled and replied jovially while giving the receipt to Natalie.

Mirzya was optimistic. She was a woman with hopes. No matter what situation lay ahead, she would always maintain her grit and calmness.

Today, they had customers before the opening of the restaurant. This was quite unusual for both of them. They usually took two hours for all the preparations so that they didn't have to take much time for each order delivery.

(The crowd was a fair indication that the restaurant was doing enough business in the neighborhood.)

Natalie took the receipt reflecting on Mirzya's smile. She took the prepared falafel from the fridge and started preparing the falafel shawarma.

Natalie came to the neighborhood 13 months back. She excelled in the art of cooking. Her food was the talk of the town. Most of her cooking she learnt from her husband whom she lost during the war. She, somehow, managed to flee the war-torn country, leaving her beautiful home behind. During her time at the restaurant, she would often dream of him standing next to her helping her, teaching her. Most of her memories were mere fragments of the time spent with her husband in their homeland. The restaurant soon became a nostalgic place for her that reminded her of the beautiful memories she cherished with him. Now, she was considered a refugee in the neighborhood.

The neighborhood had given refuge to a few such families who survived the war. She was only accompanied by her 7-year-old son. She still was carrying the papers as a reminder that the land she was currently residing in, didn't belong to her. Natalie would diligently remind herself that she was a foreign, without a miss.

Ch. 4

The Bonded Labor ?

"Jafar, is the shipment to Ashdod done?" "It was supposed to be done yesterday. "

The shipment is ready but…. There are some technical challenges. The server was down, so we couldn't put the details of the shipment.

"So, I had to hold the shipment and probably we will have to hold it for today," Jafar said casually.

Jafar's manager Danniyel replied in an affirmative tone, "It can't wait any longer…."

And, the details could have been put even after the shipment, right?

Jafar listened to his boss silently, with his head down. With embarrassment in his eyes and a great hesitation in his speech, he moved to the right of his desk and came out of his cabin to ask his team when the shipment would be loaded from the godown.

Jafar worked in an office near his home. To be precise, it was only a stone's throw away from his house. His office dealt with textile and home craft businesses where Jafar was appointed as a supervisor, taking care of the shipments, and loads and keeping track of everything. Although, he was supervising the shipments to all parts of the country, he was paid peanuts only to be compensated through free food at work. Still, he preferred bringing his lunch and snacks, prepared by Mirzya.

He got his own cabin, a desk, a locker, book racks to keep documents, and lastly a small antiquated desktop computer. Jafar was grossly derelict in his duties. He often would be seen goofing off and giving excuses. It wouldn't be wrong to judge him for his work ethic which was the complete opposite of Mirzya.

Ch. 5
The Respect

"Ima, I chose this." Danniyel took out the shoes and showed them to his mother. He said happily that I got this from Abiram's uncle's shop.

Ima gave her legs with a frown face. After wearing the shoes, she immediately removed them and said in a berated tone "I don't need shoes."

"Imaa.. what happened?" "Didn't you like it?"

"Have you seen the color?" "It's not pink."

Danniyel took the shoes with his eyes misted up. He packed them back the same way he brought them for her Ima. Derora, Danniyel's wife, was watching all this from behind the bedroom door. She was very sentimental. She wanted to console her husband but she couldn't. Danniyel while leaving saw her wife gently and sadly.

Her mother-in-law saw Derora and said in a much harsher tone than she could ever have, "Did you dry my clothes?"

She held her head down and rushed to hang the clothes.

While hanging the cloth outside their home on the right side of the front yard, Danniyel, standing at the main gate grieving, saw Derora. They both saw each other with immense sadness in their eyes, feeling pity for each other. With a heavy heart, he turned his eyes to leave for Abiram's uncle's shop. He was carrying the shoe bag in his hands.

Danniyel was a kind man, but a man with principles. He served as the Procurement and Shipment Manager. His house was in the same neighborhood as Mirzya. The house was built long back by his father. It had a village touch with a big front yard filled with shabby grasses and bushes, some even turned golden. The house was a two-storied building just like Mirzya's. The house was filled with antique types of furniture. Even the kitchen utensils were old-fashioned telling the story that the house never saw anything new. Perhaps,

Derora didn't have much privilege to call it her own home. She married Danniyel 7 years back. Whenever she tried to decorate, renovate, or bring something new to the home, she was shut down by Danniyel's mother. She, now, had learned to live her life as it is. Although Danniyel and Derora still shared a deep love for one another, over time, an unspoken distance slowly developed between them in their marriage.

Ch. 6

The Desire and The Hope

It was the next day at the restaurant. Natalie was cleaning the kitchen and finishing her work.

Natalie… one last shawarma with extra hummus. Also, Here are the keys, Mirzya took out the keys from the cash counter drawer and gave them to Natalie.

I have already cleaned and arranged the tables. Go home soon. Good night, she told her everything in one go. She had a pleasant smile on her face.

Natalie looked at the keys and pondered over something for a bit. She paused and then started preparing the order. Mirzya on her way back walked over the bridge to reach the nearby market. Today, she chose to pass the sitting near the bridge.

Walking through the market, her eyes stopped at the crochet woven winter caps for her two little girls. While looking at the caps for her girls, her eyes stumbled upon a golden scarf hanging through the hanger stand. She took the scarf and stroked it very gently before putting it on. She looked shyingly at herself in the mirror wearing the golden scarf. She took her scarf out of her head smiling, folding it in a rumpled way, and going straight to the billing counter to join the queue. She was happy. She couldn't stop stroking the scarf. She put forth the caps and the scarf and waited patiently for the shopkeeper to give the billing. It's 411.82 New Shekel. She found herself dumbstruck. She understood that she would have to leave the golden scarf. She kept it aside at the billing counter. She asked the shopkeeper to re-calculate. She had a look at the scarf, quickly turned to pay the bill, took the caps that were placed inside the bag, and left. Disappointed, she looked at the scarf one last time from outside the glass window that was still lying on the side of the billing counter. Her desire for the golden scarf ended there.

She reached home, opened the house door, kept her shoes on the side, and hung her coat. She was about to go to the living and dining room when her two daughters and her son came running calling Imaaaa.... She hugged them and told her daughters that she had a surprise for them.

Come, let's open your surprises on the sofa. Her mother-in-law was sitting in the hall. She showed them the caps and tried the beautiful caps on them.

After seeing her kids and their joy, she joined them, letting go of her desire to wear something other than black. She was at ease.

"Imi, where is my surprise?" Her son asked. She looked at him lovingly and put him in his lap. She took out the Parra Chocholate from her bag which was her son's favorite.

"I will get you the cap, once you tore it." She said tickling her son. All laughed and enjoyed the moment together. She forgot all her worries.

Jafar will be coming home. Her mother-in-law hinted that her time of gratification was over. She needs to start dinner preparation.

She saw the clock. It was 8:30 pm. She left her kids asking them to play and got herself ready to go to the kitchen.

Natalie was preparing to close the restaurant. She went ahead to put the receipt of the last order where she saw money collected for the day. She paused for a bit… as if she was tempted from within. Something inside her was bothering and compelling her to take the money. The compulsion to take the cash was so intense that she almost had a hold of it. She was filled with anger, and grief thinking that she didn't want to be gaped by her landlord anymore. She closed her eyes, looked at the cash, and decided to nod in disagreement with herself, keeping her lips closed. Perhaps her morality on what she would tell Mirzya who trusted her so much, pushed her to close the drawer. She switched off the lights, took the keys to lock the restaurant, and headed towards her home. She adjusted the long sleeves of her coat and put on her winter cap. It was snowy, which was quite unusual.

Ch. 7

The Helplessness

Jafar entered the kitchen. "Where is your scarf?" Mirzya was cooking bread with her hair tied up.

"Cooking must be done with a scarf." Jafar kept the coffee mug in the sink while lecturing her on the rules and nuisances of modesty.

At the table, food was served.

Abba, cap, cap, little girls pointed at their heads showing their caps to Jafar.

"Who brought you this?" Jafar, a little annoyed, yet in a playful tone asked the kids.

"Imaa..", one of the daughters innocently replied with an ecstatic voice pointing towards Mirzya who was going back and forth between the kitchen and hall to plate the dinner.

Kids, start your dinner. Mirzya said while keeping the last plate of hummus. They were playing in one corner of the hall. It was utterly evident that she was not paying any heed to Jafar's talks. Jafar enquired about the pink scarf that the girls already had. Mirzya, while serving to Jafar and others said in a lighter tone that both got torn. Jafar looked towards his mother and said "These days jobs are very unpredictable. We need to save more. "

"Hand over the restaurant money to Ima."

While the conversation was still on, Mirzya finished serving food, pulled the chair, and sat. She remained quiet and concentrated on her food. It would have been quite unusual if she reverted to him.

It was the next morning. The weather was quite sunny for a morning winter.

Danniyel reached the office. In his head, a few thoughts were perturbing him. One of the staff members stood up from his desk, went straight to Danniyel's office running and said

"Danniyel, two of our shipments went missing. They did not get delivered to clients. "

Danniyel put his bag on his desk, took a deep breath, and rushed in anger towards Jafar. Jafar sitting in his cabin guessed the reason behind Danniyel's anger. He stood up from his seat before Danniyel even opened the glass door of his cabin.

Before Danniyel could have said something, Jafar said with a little trembling, "I am working on it with priority."

"I need immediate answers. Fix your mess, Jafar." "This is your last chance. I need to answer the clients. " Danniyel's both tone and pitch were high. Jafar listened to Danniyel's admonishment until he left. Jafar, shell-shocked and stressed, started working.

Although Jafar portrayed himself as a firm and authoritative man in front of his family, he felt and behaved very timidly, and often got intimidated at his workplace. It would not be wrong to say that he was underconfident.

Natalie was waiting outside a small school. The school was specifically for refugee kids. Her son came running. She happily put her arms around his shoulders. They both headed towards their home conversing "What did you learn today?"

The school was established as part of the neighborhood. It provided work, shelter, and school for the kids of many refugees in the neighborhood. However, there were still many refugees who were circling the government office to get the papers.

The sunny day passed, and the clouds turned into a deep shade of blood-red color reflecting from every corner of the sky. It was still a beautiful evening.

Mirzya was at the restaurant, busy preparing, billing, and taking care of the orders. After the last order, she arranged the napkins, and salt and pepper shakers. Generally, she would keep them near the order-receiving counter which was far left of the billing counter.

She went inside the kitchen and told Natalie good night, gave the keys, and left with a smile.

Mirzya while going her way back home saw a poster reflecting the title

"A 60-day course on media and journalism for women of our community".

Mirzya paused for a while, then immediately took out her phone and took a snap of the poster. She continued her walk to her home.

It was the next morning outside the asbestos-spread roof of a tiny house.

"Here is the rest amount." Natalie handed over 500 to her landlord.

"Next month, no installments," Kiev spoke strongly while keeping the money in his pocket.

Natalie saw him with a calm face giving hardly any expression. Her son came from inside peeping through her left hand which was still holding the left side of the door.

Ch. 8

The Night Before the Storm

"Where is the shipment?" Danniyel asked.

"I am trying my best to close this by today."

"Clients won't wait, Jafar."

"I will give you an update soon."

Jafar worked the whole night in the office. Probably, he understood that it was his last chance.

The next morning at 7:00 am he rang the doorbell. Mirzya opened the door.

"This time?" Jafar asked annoyingly.

Mirzya was ready to go to the restaurant.

"Today will be more crowded, so I thought of opening early and doing the preparations."

"It's Sunday, so..." Mirzya stopped before completing the sentence but she maintained her calmness.

"I need coffee," Jafar spoke in an orderly tone while he entered the house from the right side of Mirzya where she was standing. She moved aside a bit.

She closed the door. Of course, she was sad but 'who' cares...

(They both entered inside, indicating that she went back to the kitchen to prepare coffee for him.)

The grasses and bushes turned golden as they were dying. It indeed was the old house of Danniyel.

"Do you know...?" "The other neighbour also put a lift for his mother. Some parents are very lucky. She gets all the respect and care that she deserves."

"Don't know what karma I did that I need to even ask for a cup of coffee." She said while taking coffee from Derora.

Danniyel was getting ready for the office. He was trying to adjust his tie standing near the mirror of the bedroom which was straight in front of the hall.

He was all ears to Ima's complaints. Saddened, he couldn't do much about it. This was the third time where his mother asked for a lift to be installed in the house. Danniyel's house was a double-storeyed building which was built by his father during the 1970s. Danniyel tried enquiring about lift installation inside the house but every electrician warned him that he first needed to change the wiring before its installation as the house is very old. The house needed a complete renovation. Danniyel was trying for a loan and filled out the mortgage application form as well but his income proof was not enough to apply for the loan which he requested for. Even though he was a manager at a shipment company, the salary was not enough for the amount of loan that he needed for renovation. Still, he didn't give up and was trying to renovate the house in parts.

Derora rushed to the kitchen to put the breakfast on the table for Danniyel.

(It was evident from the morning chaos that she was rushing to feed everyone in the house except herself. She hardly used to speak, and some people in the neighborhood would often mistake her as dumb. She was the center of the gossip in the neighborhood where people would assume her to be sterile. Because of these rumors, people refrained from coming to Danniyel's house. However, Derora would keep her silence, perhaps she had a better understanding of society and societal norms.

Natalie was playing with her kid when her 7-year-old son asked.

"Ima, why don't we have a refrigerator?"

"Why refrigerator?" Natalie was quite surprised at his son's question. Why was a small kid asking specifically for a refrigerator?

"I get hungry till you come back from work. " she didn't have any answer for his son. She got very emotional and immediately hugged her son.

"Natalie had been struggling to make ends meet since they became refugees. Her house, which was asbestos-roofed, was charged by Kiev 500 New Shekel more just because they were refugees. However, Mirzya would usually let her take some food from the restaurant. However, Natalie would ensure that she avoids taking anything from the restaurant except… for her wages."

"We will have it soon," Natalie replied, wiping her tears.

"Is it?" Her kid asked in an ecstatic tone. Both smiled and continued playing.

Ch. 9

The Night and The Turn

Both Mirzya and Natalie were busy preparing and arranging at the restaurant. They had a habit of pre-cooking and keeping. Generally, they pre-cooked hummus, falafel, grilled chicken, grilled beef, and tahini. In fact, Natalie would bake the bread in the oven and keep it ready.

"I am thinking… I will join a free journalism course which is being offered to the community for free." Mirzya mentioned Natalie.

Natalie while arranging the bread loaves asked with curiosity "What is it ?"

She mentioned the 60-day workshop for media journalism while cleaning the microwave. "I am thinking of joining their editor class."

"There is so much to write about." She said in a very despondent tone. She remembered faint pictures of how she had been put as a secondary at her home. Her husband's taunts, complaints, and patriarchal beliefs, her mother-in-law's silence, and her own silence because of the kids ' future. Her mother-in-law was well aware of Jafar's behaviour towards Mirzya. She disapproved of his son's behaviour, but instead of confronting Jafar, she chose to blindfold herself.

Needless to mention, it must have been a fight for Mirzya to work at the restaurant. Probably, they allowed her to work to feed the family.

"Mirzya, … Mirzya". Natalie called her twice. She came out of her thoughts and asked, "Did you…Did you say something?"

"When are you thinking of joining?" Natalie asked.

"From today", she replied smilingly while folding the hand towel.

Natalie smiled back. She seemed very happy for her.

But she paused and suddenly asked, "Who will be at the restaurant then?" Mirzya did not have an answer. She was surprised though at the question. She forgot about the restaurant. She was all confused and puzzled but didn't have an answer to her question.

It was almost night and the weather was still cold. Mirzya was about to leave when she called Natalie.

"Natalie, I have kept the keys near the counter." "Today is my first day." She looked at Natalie who was working in the kitchen.

"I have cleaned and arranged the empty tables," Mirzya said exhaling a few breaths.

Natalie smiled and wished good luck to her.

Danniyel barged into Jafar's cabin with a few papers and asked Jafar to show the papers which contained labeling; these two shipments were also delivered to the wrong locations.

He put forth the papers containing the labels to Jafar.

Jafar took the labels in fear.

"Jafar, I cannot have this more."

" It's time, go home. "

This time, Danniyel said in a very calm tone. Jafar understood the situation, still, he was completely startled.

Derora was preparing dinner when her mother-in-law asked her to iron her clothes as tomorrow she was going out with her neighbours to pluck oranges.

Derora left the dinner preparations and rushed to iron her clothes.

Mirzya went to journalism classes where she found a big queue. Here is the registration form for the classes, a boy came running and put a form in her hands. It happened in a flash that Mirzya was left bewildered. Her eyes started searching in the crowd for the boy who gave her the form, but all in vain. She couldn't understand the event that just happened and thought of looking at the form. She glanced at the form and searched for a pen inside her bag. As she started to fill out the form, she realized that the registration fee cost was 5500 New Shekel. This time, she started searching diligently amidst the rush for the person who gave her the form. Finally, she found him sitting on a chair with forms lying on the front bench.

But it was mentioned free, Mirzya asked all puzzled and startled by putting the form on the bench showing the registration fee cost section of the form.

"Yes, madam. The course and materials provided.... such as free laptop access, stationary, and library access, all are free. Butttt... registration charges, it's there."

"How is the course fee different from the registration fee?" Mirzya said in a feeble voice. She paused for a moment before confronting the guy that she didn't have enough money.

"I don't...don't have that much money right now."

"Can I come tomorrow?" This time Mirzya was very nervous.

"Yes, madam." "Registration is open till Sunday. You have a week's time." After saying this, he got busy with handing over registration forms, billing for students who paid the money, and so forth.

Mirzya left for her home downhearted. She almost got tears in her eyes, but being Mirzya, the strong-headed woman, she walked towards her home normally as if nothing shattered for her. But her heart knew about her feelings that were screaming to let her out of the bondage and have her own choice.

Natalie was still at the restaurant calculating and keeping the rest of the receipts. She opened the drawer to keep them where she saw the cash. However, she nodded no within herself and closed the cash drawer. She switched off the lights and opened the main door of the restaurant to head towards her home.

Mirzya had a second thought while going back to her home. She thought of going to the restaurant to get the money to pay for the registration fees. She turned back and rushed towards the restaurant only to find out that Natalie had closed the restaurant. She immediately realized that there would be a pair of keys in her handbag that she always keeps. She started searching for the keys inside her handbag. She was fortunate to find them. She quickly looked for the key to the restaurant's main door. She opened the restaurant and quickly took the money from the billing counter drawer. She rushed towards the place where registration was happening only to find that the course fee counter had been closed. Disappointed, she headed towards her home.

Mirzya, who felt as if something again had been snatched away from her by her fate, opened her house door. She was a little surprised to see Jafar, who was waiting at the dinner. Jafar usually would not be home this soon.

She sensed the tension that was quite evident on Jafar's face. She moved slowly towards the dining table.

"Sit here, I need to talk," Jafar asked her in a commanding voice. Tomorrow, I will be going to the restaurant. He tried to leave the dining table to go to his room.

"What happened?" "Are you not going to your job tomorrow?" She asked, sitting on the dining chair keeping her bag on her lap. She was looking at everyone's face in perplexity.

"It's no longer." He replied in a sordid tone.

"From tomorrow, you will take care of the house and family. "

But…we both can take care of the restaurant…. She replied desperately.

She couldn't ask further about his workplace and what happened to his job. Perhaps, she understood.

"Natalie is there to help." Jafar cut her off with his argument.

She tried to beg Jafar but ended up weeping all by herself. Her kids surrounded her wondering what just happened. She couldn't resist her tears and said in tears, "The restaurant is the only happy place for me." Jafar was getting up from the dining chair.

"Why? Is family, this house, not a happy place?"

"It's already 8:30 pm. We all are waiting for dinner." Jafar, as usual, didn't pay any heed to her feelings, emotions, and even her cry.

She didn't get a chance to mourn over her loss of freedom. She knew very well that this was the end, the end of her dream. The restaurant was not just a place where she used to work, but it was a place of hopes, dreams, and memories of her childhood. A place that provided her with a sense of being herself. Deep within her, she was screaming that the restaurant was hers, yet no one was there to hear her scream or her cry.

She went to the kitchen with a heavy heart. But it didn't take her much time to come to her normalcy to start preparing dinner. That night she prepared her kid's favorite al-faham, baked bread, and chickpea hummus.

Natalie was walking through the second-hand market when she saw a small grey color fridge. She stopped by to enquire about the price.

"It's 350." The shopkeeper replied.

"Can it be 300?"

"Delivery address" ... put it here. The shop owner told her while forwarding pen and paper. She ecstatically started writing her house address.

It was the big lawn with old, dried bushes, some of which turned golden.

"Aah, what a start to the morning. The oranges this season have come really well. "

"Adele's daughter-in-law makes amazing shakshuka." After a long time, I had an appetite."

Derora was listening to everything but preferred to remain silent. She forwarded the coffee to her mother-in-law.

"Danniyel..., are you listening?" "This is why no guests come to our house. Nobody asks for even a cup of coffee here." Mother-in-law stared at Derora while taking the coffee from her hands. Derora after offering coffee left without saying a word.

She went to the bedroom where Danniyel was getting ready for the office. Derora entered the room.

"Danniyel, I wish to talk."

"Ya, tell." Danniyel innocently asked.

"I cannot have this anymore."

"I didn't understand. What happened?"

"I don't think I am capable of making people happy or…anyone happy."

"I need some time." Derora broke in front of Danniyel.

"Dero…, please don't take Ima's words to your heart."

"You know her." Danniyel tried to calm her down. He usually called her 'Dero'.

"I want a home, Danniyel."

Those words made Danniyel stop. He understood.

Danniyel was a very kind and genuine person. Above all, her love for Derora was immense. He didn't say much to stop her. But Danniyel and Derora saw each other with love one last time.

She left the house and started staying with her Aunt. Danniyel was standing near the hall watching her go. His mother asked him what happened.

"Why is she with her bags? "

Danniyel with tears in his eyes told his mother that she was going home.

His mother made absurd faces and went to her room. Danniyel was still standing feeling helpless.

Mirzya came to bed after serving dinner and washing utensils. She saw her bag lying half-opened on the side table where 5500 New Shekel for the registration fee along with the form was quite visible. She kept on staring at it standing near it, lamenting over her destiny. Her eyes were filled with tears. She went to the bed, removed her scarf, and hung it next to the bedside table.

That night Mirzya couldn't sleep. For her, as if the whole world became upside down. Whatever little she had for herself, she lost it that night.

Natalie asked 'Stop… stop… stop here'. The shop owner stopped the vehicle. Natalie came out of the vehicle.

"Please be careful."

"This way."

"Keep it here."

He puts the refrigerator outside her house. She opened her house door. Her kid came running to Ima and hugged her.

She asked happily, "Do you want ice cream?" The kid nodded, smiling. "Go outside and check."

"Aa.. Imaaaa…", he ran and hugged her. He was so excited.

"Let's make some ice cream," Natalie said. Both of them seemed happy after a long time.

Her landlord after hearing voices came out and shouted,

"When are you paying rent?"

"Tomorrow will give Mr. Kiev." Natalie sounded so confident making Kiev stunned.

He was so surprised at how for the first time she was so confident. He murmured within himself "Has she got any lottery?"

Natalie went inside with her kid.

Ch. 10

The Real Bonded Laborers

The next morning, Jafar was seen leaving for the restaurant reminding Mirzya who was standing at the door hoping things would change someday.

Natalie had already opened the restaurant and was washing utensils.

Jafar asked Natalie for all receipts from the previous month.

Natalie was surprised upon seeing Jafar. She looked here and there and asked him.

"Where is Mirzya?"

"She is home." Jafar replied with his eyes down at the cash counter looking for accounts' registers.

He looked up at Natalie and asked

"Can I get all receipts and accounts logs ?"

She brought those and kept them on the table. She was still puzzled about what happened and tried to enquire.

"Is Mirzya okay?" "Is she sick?"

It was the rarest of the days when Mirzya would not come.

Jafar didn't answer and made himself engrossed in the receipts calculation. He pulled out the calculator and started putting numbers as if he didn't pay any heed to her questions.

Jafar spent the entire day calculating receipts of the orders made in the previous month. He checked the money count was 15757.50 but only 9557.50 was in the bill counter drawer.

Natalie, did we pay the electricity bill already?

"For the previous month?" Natalie asked surprisingly.

"Yes." Jafar replied in a very rude way.

"No, I haven't. I don't think Mirzya has also paid the bill. "

"But there is a discrepancy in the count."

"Only 9557.50 is left. The total revenue is 15757.50. "

Out of fear, she told him abruptly that she didn't know much about accounts.

"Mirzya handled the accounts."

Jafar sensed something. She looked suspicious to Jafar as she trembled while stating that accounts were not her department to handle at the restaurant.

"If the electricity bill is pending, EMI for the restaurant appliances is also not logged in this register, then.... where did the money go?"

"I... I don't know." "How should I know?" She said while making dough for the bread. Her eyes were balling here and there.

"Natalie, are you hiding something?" "Because EB will not be this high even if paid and not logged in the register," Jafar asked politely which was unusual for his personality. He was holding the register in his hands.

She was panicking. Her hands were trembling.

"I don't understand what you are talking about."

Jafar got suspicious seeing Natalie's behavior.

"You have something to tell me." "Don't hide", Natalie.

She was muttering something upon which he asked "What are you saying?"

"I only took 700."

He quickly turned from this temporary polite man to his actual self. In anger, he rebuked her and asked her to leave. He firmly guided her to refrain from coming to the restaurant from thereon.

"Do not step inside this restaurant."

"Jafar, please don't do this. I was about to tell Mirzya." Natalie requested and pleaded with him.

He took her bag, held her hand, and forcefully walked her out of the restaurant.

"Jafar.. Jafar Jafar, please." "Please don't do this. I was in need. I would have told Mirzya. You can cut from my salary." He turned towards the restaurant. She ran behind him frightened at the fact that she was left with no work. How would she feed her kid?

"What about the other 5500?" He turned and asked her while opening the restaurant door.

"I.. I have a kid."

"Leave..." He said while closing the restaurant door from inside.

She was standing outside the restaurant door speechless, her face was begging him to forgive and give her a chance.

Until she realized that he would not change his mind. With her face down, tears rolling down her cheeks, she left. She headed towards her house.

Natalie closed the restaurant door and left. Just a few steps ahead, she remembered what her son asked that morning. She went back to the restaurant, and without giving much thought to her morality, she took 700 New Shekel from the bill counter drawer. She did have a thought, though, that she would inform Mirzya the very first thing in the morning.

She closed the restaurant door again and headed towards her home. It was after this incident that Mirzya came running back where she found the restaurant closed. She immediately looked for a second pair of keys inside her handbag and took 5500 New Shekel for the registration fee.)

"You can't live here longer." Derora's Aunt mentioned to her to look for a place for herself. She said bluntly that she could not afford to stay for a long period. Derora listened to everything silently, took her bag at the same moment, and left to search for a house in the neighborhood. She didn't have money, yet it was the first time Derora took a step for her self-worth.

It was very late at night at Mirzya's home.

At the dinner table, Jafar mentioned to her Immi that he asked Natalie to leave as he found her taking money from the restaurant.

"That's why you need males to handle jobs." Jafar was a little loud when Mirzya was keeping the plates at the table.

She was listening to everything. She wanted to say many things, about Natalie and how good she was, about Jafar's behaviour and her misery, yet again she chose to remain silent. Perhaps, she either gave up on her life or she had a hope that one day, maybe one day, she would manage her restaurant again. She probably would amend the things and bring back Natalie.

Derora was sleeping under a huge tree that had been standing for ages. Abiram's uncle saw her and asked her to stay at his place.

She would go out in search of a job so that she could afford to rent a place. She stopped by Mirzya's restaurant where a "Helper Required" board was hung at the door. She went inside the restaurant without giving much of a thought.

"Hello", she said to Jafar who was at the billing counter.

Jafar while looking at her computer asked

"What shall we get for you, madam?"

"Outside, it's written helper is required."

It's for kitchen work. Jafar answered normally.

"I can do," Derora replied in a hurry.

"Do you know how to make and plate shawarma?"

"Yeah…" She nodded her head.

"Salary is 1200. I can't pay more."

She again nodded her head in agreement. Being an uneducated woman who never stepped out of the house, didn't know much about wages.

"You can start from today." The tables need to be arranged and then bread needs to be prepared.

She put her bag in the corner. With a smile on her face as if she had got her freedom, she went ahead to arrange the tables.

Jafar reached home where food was ready to be served on the dining table. It was 7:30 pm.

She looked sad. He saw her, very well noticed her sadness but instead of comforting her, gave her a lunch box to keep.

While getting ready for the next morning, he saw Mirzya's form of journalism and money inside her handbag. He gently took out the form and noticed the fee amount of 5500. He took out the money from the bag hastily. He understood everything.

Mirzya entered the room. She saw the form and money in his hands.

"So, it was you." "When were you planning to tell me?"

She could not say a word.

"Never ever think of the restaurant again." "You had enough freedom to misuse it."

"She stayed silent with no expression on her face."

Derora was roaming around the community to find a place, mostly a room on a sharing basis.

She saw a board outside an asbestos house stating "Need a female member for sharing a room." Derora knocked on the door.

The door was opened. It was Natalie on the other side.

"Yesss..?" Natalie asked.

"Is the room still available?" Derora asked.

"Yes, it's 500 for the sharing. "

"I can pay 400."

"Come, I will show you the house," Natalie replied.

Ch. 11

The Restaurant as a "He"

A year passed… It was a cozy winter again.

Mirzya put on her scarf, and her coat, packed the lunch box, and went towards the restaurant. She opened the door and put the lunch box near the billing counter where Jafar was sitting near the computer.

She was looking in and out of the restaurant. So much had changed in 1 year. She was coming to the restaurant after a year gap. She saw the walls, the European-style paintings were removed, and the wall was painted blank. The restaurant's color was faded.

"Why are you here?"

"You asked for home food. Today you left early, so came to give you a lunch box." Mirzya spoke confidently without fear. This time she was not so silent. Perhaps, she accepted that she had nothing more to lose.

"Okay, you can leave now," Jafar spoke in a careless tone.

She tried to peep in the kitchen where she found Derora was preparing chicken shawarma. She was all tired and handling everything all by herself.

"Mirzya.. Mirzya", Jafar said her name in a loud voice the second time.

"Hmm".. He gave her a signal by showing the restaurant door.

She didn't question his behavior, just smiled and left. After all, it was her restaurant but she preferred quietness.

"Derora, keep the napkins." Jafar scolded Derora. She rushed to keep the napkins and went back to the kitchen to prepare the order.

"What about order no 15? Shakshuka?" Jafar chided her.

"It's done." Scared, Derora replied.

"Serve the table," Jafar ordered and went near the cash counter to sit. Perhaps Jafar didn't learn his lesson from his last job. He still preferred to sit.

She took the order and served it to Table No. 15.

"Hello, Dero..." Derora turned towards the voice. She was not surprised seeing Danniyel. He was coming to the restaurant every Sunday just to have a glimpse of her, disguising himself so that Jafar didn't find out. His love was the sole comfort Derora had left. Deep down Danniyel knew that she wasn't coming back, yet, he found himself returning only to check on her if she was alright.

While coming out of the restaurant, Mirzya saw Natalie on the opposite side of the road where she was standing, watching the restaurant from afar. Both of them saw each other, without speaking a word or making an effort to have any expressions on their face. But empathy for each other's misery was visible on their faces. Mirzya felt pity for Derora too who was working as a bonded laborer for Jafar. But she felt helpless. Both Mirzya and Natalie felt helpless for themselves and each other.

They perhaps understood that if they hadn't turned back that night, they both would have enjoyed their little world of happiness.

Mirzya noticed a pack of clothes and a stitching kit in Natalie's hands which made her understand that she had got a job at some cloth production factory.

They stood locked in a silent gaze, each wondering if, on the day of registration, they had not turned toward the restaurant, their story might have unfolded differently—perhaps even better than the one they now lived in.

After a long silence, they both decided to walk in opposite directions accepting the paths their lives had taken. This time, they didn't see the restaurant that was once their "own". Perhaps, the restaurant was no longer a nostalgic place for either of them.